he telling or reading of ghost stories during long, dark and cold Christmas nights is a yuletide ritual which dates to at least the eighteenth century, and was once as much a part of Christmas tradition as decorating fir trees, feasting on goose and the singing of carols. During the Victorian era many magazines printed ghost stories specifically for the Christmas season. These "winter tales" did not necessarily explore Christmas themes in any manner. Rather, they were offered as an eerie pleasure to be enjoyed on Christmas eve with the family, adding a supernatural shiver to the seasonal chill.

This tradition remained strong in the British Isles (and her colonies) throughout much of the twentieth century, though in recent years it has been on the wane. Certainly, few people in Canada or the United States seem to know about it any longer. This series of small books seeks to rectify this, to revive a charming custom for the long, dark nights we all know so well here at Christmastime.

THE HAUNTED BOOKSHELF

THE GREEN ROOM

THE GREEN ROOM

E.F.

WALTER DE LA MARE

A GHOST STORY FOR CHRISTMAS

DESIGNED & DECORATED BY SETH

BIBLIOASIS

Only Mr. Elliott's choicer customers were in his own due season let into his little secret—namely, that at the far end of his shop—beyond, that is, the little table on which he kept his account books, his penny bottle of ink and his rusty pen, there was an annexe. He first allowed his victims to ripen; and preferred even to see their names installed in the pages of his fat dumpy ledger before he decided that they were really worthy of this little privilege.

Alan, at any rate, though a young man of ample leisure and moderate means, had been browsing and pottering about on and off in the shop for weeks before he even so much as suspected there *was* a hidden door. He must, in his innocence, have spent pounds and pounds on volumes selected from the vulgar shelves before his own initiation.

This was on a morning in March. Mr. Elliott was tying up a parcel for him. Having no scissors handy he was burning off the ends of the string with a lighted match. And as if its small flame had snapped at the same moment both the string and the last strands of formality between them, he glanced up almost roguishly at the young man through his large round spectacles with the remark, "P'raps, sir, you would like to take a look at the books in the parlour?" And a bird-like jerk of his round bald head indicated where the parlour was to be found.

Alan had merely looked at him for a moment or two out of his blue eyes with his usual pensive vacancy. "I didn't know there *was* another room," he said at last. "But then, I suppose it wouldn't have occurred to me to think there might be. I fancied these books were all the books you had.' He glanced over the dingy hugger-mugger of second-hand literature that filled the shelves and littered the floor—a mass that would have twenty-fold justified the satiety of a Solomon.

"Oh, dear me, no, sir," said Mr. Elliott, with the pleasantest confidentiality. "All this is chiefly riff-raff. But I don't mention it except to those gentlemen who are old clients, in a manner of speaking. What's in there is all in the printed catalogue and I can always get what's asked for. Apart from that, there's some who—well, at any rate, I *don't*, sir. But if by any chance you should care to take a look round at any time, you would, I'm sure, be very welcome. This is an oldish house, as you may have noticed, sir, and out there are the oldest part of it. We call it the parlour—Mrs. Elliott and me; we got it from the parties that were here before we came. Take a look now, sir, if you please, it's a nice little place."

Mr. Elliott drew aside. Books—and particularly old books—tend to be dusty company. This may account for the fact that few antiquarian booksellers are of Falstaffian proportions. They are more usually lean, ruminative, dryish spectators of life. The gnawing of the worm in the tome is among the more melancholy of nature's lullabies; and the fluctuations in price of "firsts" and of "mint states" must incline any temperament if not towards cynicism, at least towards the philosophical. Herodotus tells of a race of pygmies whose only diet was the odour of roses; and though morocco leather is sweeter than roses, it is even less fattening.

Mr. Elliott, however, flourished on it. He was a rotund little man, with a silver watch-chain from which a gold locket dangled, and he had uncommonly small feet. He might have been a ballet-master. "You make your way up those four stairs, sir," he went on, as he ushered his customer beneath the curtain, "turn left down the passage, and the door's on the right. It's quiet in there, but that's no harm done. No hurry, sir."

So Alan proceeded on his way. The drugget on the passage floor showed little trace of wear. The low panelled walls had been whitewashed. He came at last to the flowered china handle of the door beyond the turn of the passage, then stood for a moment lost in surprise. But it was the trim cobbled garden beyond the square window on his right that took his glance rather than the room itself. Yellow crocuses, laden with saffron pollen, stood wide agape in the black mould; and the greening buds of a bush of lilac were tapping softly against the glass. And above was a sky of the gentlest silken blue; wonderfully still.

He turned and looked about him. The paint on wainscot and cornice must once have been of a bright apple green. It had faded now. A gate-leg table was in the far corner beyond the small-paned window; and on his left, with three shallow steps up to it, was another door. And the shelves were lined from floor to ceiling with the literary treasures which Mr. Elliott kept solely for his elect.

So quiet was the room that even the flitting of a clothes-moth might be audible, though the brightness of noonday now filled it to the brim. For the three poplars beyond the lilac bush were still almost as bare as the frosts of winter had made them.

In spite of the flooding March light, in spite of this demure sprightliness after the gloom and disorder of the shop he had left behind him, Alan—as in his languid fashion he turned his head from side to side—became conscious first and foremost or the *age* of Mr. Elliott's pretty parlour. The paint was only a sort of "Let's pretend." The space between its walls seemed, indeed, to be as much a reservoir of time as of light. The panelled ceiling, for example, was cracked and slightly discoloured; so were the green shutter-cases to the windows; while the small and beautiful chimney-piece—its carved marble lintel depicting a Cupid with pan pipes dancing before a smiling goddess under a weeping willow—enshrined a grate that at this moment contained nothing, not even the ashes of a burnt-out fire. Its bars were rusty, and there were signs of damp in the moulded plaster above it.

A gentle breeze was now brisking the tops of the poplar trees, but no murmur of it reached Alan where he stood. With his parcel tucked under his arm, he edged round softly from shelf to shelf and even

after so cursory an examination as this—
and it was one of Mr. Elliott's principles
to mark all his books in plain figures—he
realized that his means were much too
moderate for his appetite. He came to a
standstill, a little at a loss. What was he to
do next? He stifled a yawn. Then, abstract-
ing a charming copy of *Hesperides*, by that
"Human and divine" poet, Robert Herrick,
he seated himself idly on the edge of the
table and began to turn over its leaves.
They soon became vocal:

> *Aske me, why I do not sing*
> *To the tension of the string,*
> *As I did not long ago,*
> *When my numbers full did flow?*
> *Griefe (ay me!) hath struck my Lute*
> *And my tongue—at one time—mute.*

His eye strayed on, and he read slowly—
muttering the words to himself as he did
so—"*The departure of the good Dæmon*":

> *What can I do in Poetry,*
> *Now the good Spirit's gone from me?*

Why nothing now, but lonely sit,
And over-read what I have writ.

Alan's indolence was even more extreme; he was at this moment merely over-reading what he had *read*—and what he had read again and again and again. For the eye may be obedient while the master of the mind sits distrait and aloof. His wits had gone wool-gathering. He paused, then made yet another attempt to fix his attention on the sense of this simple quatrain. But in vain. For in a moment or two his light clear eyes had once more withdrawn themselves from the printed page and were once more, but now more intently, exploring the small green room in which he sat.

And as he did so—though nothing of the bright external scene around him showed any change—out of some daydream, it seemed, of which until then he had been unaware, there had appeared to him from the world of fantasy the image of a face.

No known or remembered face—a phantom face, as alien and inscrutable as are the apparitions that occasionally visit the mind in sleep. This in itself was not a very unusual experience. Alan was a young man of an imaginative temperament, and possessed that inward eye which is often, though not unfailingly, the bliss of solitude. And yet there was a difference. This homeless image was at once so real in effect, so clear, and yet so unexpected. Even the faint shadowy colours of the features were discernible—the eyes dark and profound, the hair drawn back over the rather narrow temples of the oval head; a longish, quiet, intent face, veiled with reverie and a sort of vigilant sorrowfulness, and yet possessing little of what at first sight might be called beauty—or what at least is usually accepted as beauty.

So many and fleeting, of course, are the pictures that float into consciousness at the decoy of a certain kind of poetry that one hardly heeds them as they pass and fade. But this, surely, was no after-image of one of Herrick's earthly yet ethereal Electras or Antheas or Dianemes, vanishing like the rainbows in a fountain's falling waters. There are degrees of realization. And, whatever "good Sprit" this shadowy visitant may have represented, and whatever its origin, it had struck *some* "observer" in Alan's mind mute indeed, and had left him curiously disquieted. It was as if in full sight of a small fishing smack peacefully becalmed beneath the noonday blue, the spars and hulk of some such phantom as the *Flying Dutchman* had suddenly appeared upon the smooth sea green; though this perhaps was hardly a flattering account of it. Anyhow, it had come, and now it was gone—except out of memory—as similar images do come and go.

Mere figment of a day-dream, then, though this vision must have been, Alan found himself vacantly searching the room as if for positive corroboration of it, or at least for some kind of evidence that would explain it away. Faces are but faces of course, whether real or imaginary, and whether they appear in the daytime or the dark, but there is at times a dweller behind the eye that looks out, though only now and again, from that small window. And *this* looker-out—unlike most—seemed to be innocent or any attempt at concealment. "Here am I... And you?" *That* had seemed to be the mute question it was asking; though with no appearance of needing an answer; and, well, Alan distrusted feminine influences. He had once or twice in his brief career loved not wisely but too idealistically, and for the time being he much preferred first editions. Besides, he disliked mixing things up—and how annoying to be first slightly elated and then chilled by a mere fancy!

The sun in his diurnal round was now casting a direct beam of light from between the poplars through one of the little panes of glass in Mr. Elliott's parlour. It limned a clear-cut shadow-pattern on the fading paint of the frame and on the floor beneath. Alan watched it and was at the same time listening—as if positively in hope of detecting that shadow's indetectable motion!

In the spell of this reverie, time seemed to have become of an almost material density. The past hung like cobwebs in the air. He turned his head abruptly; he was beginning to feel a little uneasy. And his eyes now fixed themselves on the narrow panelled door above the three stairs on the other side of the room. When consciousness is thus unusually alert it is more easily deceived by fancies. And yet so profound was the quiet around him it seemed improbable that the faint sound he had heard as of silk very lightly brushing against some material obstacle was imaginary. Was there a listener behind that door? Or was there not? If so, it must be one as intent as himself, but far more secret.

For a full minute, and as steadily as a cat crouching over a mouse's hole—though there wasn't the least trace of the predatory on his mild fair features, he scrutinized the key in the lock. He breathed again; and then with finger in book to keep his place tiptoed across the room and gently—by a mere finger's breadth—opened the door. Another moment and he had pushed it wider. Nothing there. Exactly as he had expected, of course. And yet—why at the same moment was he both disappointed and relieved?

He had exposed a narrow staircase—unstained, uncarpeted. Less than a dozen steep steps up was another door—a shut door, with yet another pretty flowered china handle and china finger-plates to it. A rather unusual staircase, too, he realized, since, unless one or other of its two doors was open, it must continually be in darkness. But you never know what oddity is going to present itself next in an old rambling house. How many human beings, he speculated, as he scanned this steep and narrow vacancy, must in the two or three centuries gone by have ascended and descended that narrow ladder—as abrupt as that of Jacob's dream? They had come disguised in the changing fashions of their time; they had gone, leaving apparently not a wrack behind.

Well, that was that. This March morning might be speciously bright and sunny but in spite of its sunshine it was cold. Books, too, may cheer the mind, but even when used as fuel they are apt to fail to warm the body, and rust on an empty grate diminishes any illusion of heat its bars might otherwise convey. Alan sighed, suddenly aware that something which had promised to be at least an arresting little experience had failed him. The phantasmal face so vividly seen, and even watched for a moment, had already become a little blurred in memory. And now there was a good deal more disappointment in his mind than relief. He felt like someone who has been cheated at a game he never intended to play. A particularly inappropriate simile, none the less, for he hadn't the smallest notion what the stakes had been, or, for that matter, what the game. He took up his hat and walking-stick, and still almost on tiptoe, and after quietly but firmly shutting both doors behind him, went back into the shop.

"I think I will take *this*, please," he said almost apologetically to the old bookseller, who with his hands under his black coat-tails was now surveying the busy world from his own doorstep.

"Certainly, sir." Mr. Elliott wheeled about and accepted the volume with that sprightly turn of his podgy wrist with which he always welcomed a book that was about to leave him forever. "Ah, the *Hesperides*, sir. I'll put the three into one parcel. A nice tall clean copy, I see. It came, if memory serves me right, from the library of Colonel Anstey, sir, who purchased the Talbot letters—and at a very reasonable price too. Now if I had a *first* in this condition!..."

Alan dutifully smiled. "I found it in the parlour," he said. "What a charming little room—and garden too; I had no idea the house was so old. Who lived in it before you did? I suppose it wasn't always a bookshop?"

He tried in vain to speak naturally and not as if he had plums in his mouth.

"Lived here before me, now?" the bookseller repeated ruminatively. "Well, sir, there was first of course my immediate predecessor. *He* came before me; and *we* took over his stock. Something of a disappointment too when I came to go through with it."

"And before *him*?" Alan persisted.

"Before him, sir? I fancy this was what might be called a *private* house. You could see if you looked round a bit how it has been converted. It was a doctor's, I understand—a Dr. Marchmont's. And what we call the parlour, sir, from which you have just emerged, was always, I take it, a sort of book room. Leastways some of the books there now were there then—with the book-plate and all. You see, the Mr. Brown who came before me and who, as I say, converted the house, *he* bought the doctor's library. Not merely medical and professional works neither. There was some choice stuff besides; and a few moderate specimens of what is known in the trade as the curious, sir. Not that I go out of my way for it, myself."

Alan paused in the doorway, parcel in hand.

"A bachelor, I suppose?"

"The doctor, sir, or Mr. Brown?"

"The doctor."

"Well now, that I couldn't rightly say," replied Mr. Elliott cheerfully. "Let us hope *not*. They tell me, sir, it makes things seem more homely-like to have a female about the house. And," he raised his voice a little,

"I'll warrant that Mrs. Elliott, sir, if she were here to say so would bear me out."

Mrs. Elliott in fact, a pasty-looking old woman, with a mouth like a cod's and a large marketing basket on her arm, was at this moment emerging out from behind a curtained doorway. Possibly her husband had caught a glimpse of her reflection in his spectacles. She came on with a beetle-like deliberation.

"What's that you were saying about me, Mr. Elliott?" she said.

"This gentleman was inquiring, my love, if Dr. Marchmont-as-was lived in a state of single blessedness or if there was a lady in the case."

Mrs. Elliott fixed a slow flat look on her husband, and then on Alan.

"There was a sister or niece or something, so they say. But I never knew anything about them, and don't want to," she declared. And Alan, a little chilled by her demeanour, left the shop.

Not that that one fish-like glance of Mrs. Elliott's censorious eye had by any means freed his fancy of what had passed.

In the days that followed he could never for an instant be sure when or where the face that reverie had somehow conjured up out of the recesses of his mind on his first visit to the old bookseller's parlour was not about to reappear. And it chose the oddest of moments. Even when his attention was definitely fixed on other things it would waft itself into his consciousness again— and always with the same serene yet vivid, naïve yet serious question in the eyes—a question surely that only life itself could answer, and that not always with a like candour or generosity. Alan was an obstinate young man in spite of appearances. But to have the rudiments of an imagination is one thing, to be at the beck and call of every passing fancy is quite another. He was not, he reassured himself, as silly as all that. He held out for days together; and then when he had been left for twenty-four hours wholly at peace—he suddenly succumbed.

A westering sun was sharply gilding its windows when he once more made his way into Mr. Elliott's parlour. It was empty. And almost at the same instant he realized how anxious he had been that this *should* be so, and how insipid a bait as such the little room now proved to be. He hadn't expected that. And yet—not exactly insipid; its flavour had definitely soured. He wished he had never come; he tried to make up his mind to go. Ill at ease, angry with himself, and as if in open defiance of some inward mentor, he took down at random a fusty old quarto from its shelf and, seating himself on a chair by the table, he began, or rather attempted, to read.

Instead, with downcast eyes shelled in by the palm of his hand, and leaning gently on his elbow in an attitude not unlike that of the slippered and pensive Keats in the portrait, he found himself listening again. He did more than listen. Every nerve in his body was stretched taut. And time ebbed away. At this tension his mind began to wander off again into a dreamlike vacuum of its own, when, "What was that?" a voice within whispered at him. A curious thrill ebbed through his body. It was as though unseen fingers had tugged at a wire—with no bell at the end of it. For this was no

sound he had heard—no stir of the air. And yet in effect it so nearly resembled one that it might have been only the sigh of the blast of the east wind at the window. He waited a minute, then, with a slight shiver, glanced up covertly but steadily through his fingers.

He was shocked—by what he saw—yet not astonished. It seemed as if his whole body had become empty and yet remained as inert and heavy as lead. He was no longer alone. The figure that stood before him in the darker corner there, and only a few paces away, was no less sharply visible and even more actual in effect than the objects around her. One hand, from a loose sleeve, resting on the edge of the door to the staircase, she stood looking at him, her right foot with its high-heeled shoe poised delicately on the lowest of the three steps. With head twisted back sidelong over her narrow shoulder, her eyes were fixed on this earthly visitor to her haunts—as he sat, hand to forehead, drawn up stiff and chill at the table. She was watching Alan. And the face, though with even fewer claims to be beautiful, and none to be better than knowing and wide-awake, was without any question the face he had shared with Herrick's *Hesperides*.

A peculiar vacancy—like a cold mist up from the sea—seemed to have spread over his mind, and yet he was alert to his very finger-tips. Had she seen he had seen her? He couldn't tell. It was as cold in the tiny room as if the windows were wide open and the garden beyond them full of snow. The late afternoon light, though bleakly clear, was already thinning away, and, victim of this silly decoy, he was a prisoner who in order to regain his freedom must pass *her* way out. He stirred in his chair, his eyes now fixed again on the book beneath them.

And then at last, as if with confidence restored, he withdrew his hand from his face, lifted his head, and affecting a boldness he far from felt, deliberately confronted his visitor. At this the expression on her features—her whole attitude—changed too. She had only at this moment seen that he had seen her, then? The arm dropped languidly to her side. Her listless body turned a little, her shoulders slightly lifted themselves, and a faint provocative smile came into her face, while the dark jaded eyes resting on his own remained half mocking, half deprecatory—almost as if the two of them, he and she, were old cronies who had met again after a long absence from one another, with ancient secrets awaiting discreet discussion. With a desperate effort Alan managed to refrain from making any answering signal of recognition. He stared back with a face as blank as a turnip. How he knew with such complete assurance that his visitor was not of this world he never attempted to explain to himself. Real! She was at least as real as a clearly lit reflection of anything seen in a looking-glass, and in *effect* on his mind was more positive than the very chair on which he was sitting and the table beneath his elbow to which that chair was drawn up. For this was a reality of the soul, and not of the senses. Indeed, he himself might be the ghost and she the dominating pervasive actuality.

But even if he had been able to speak he had no words with which to express himself. He was shuddering with cold and had suddenly become horribly fatigued and exhausted. He wanted to "get out" of all this and yet knew not only that this phantasm must have been lying in wait for him, but that sooner or later she would compel him to find out what she wanted of him, that she meant to be satisfied. Her face continued to change in expression even while he watched her. Its assurance seemed to intensify. The head stooped forward a little; the narrow pallid slanting eyelids momentarily closed; and then, with a gesture not merely of arm or shoulder but of her whole body, she once more fixed him with a gaze more intense, more challenging, more crammed with meaning than he had supposed possible in any human eye. It was as if some small wicket gate into the glooms of Purgatory had suddenly become thronged with bright-lit faces.

Until this moment they had been merely eyeing one another while time's sluggish moments ebbed away. They had been merely "looking at" one another. Now there had entered those glazed dark fixed blue eyes the very self within. It stayed there gazing out at him transfixed—the pleading, tormented, dangerous spirit within that intangible husk. And then the crisis was over. With a slow dragging movement of his head, Alan had at last succeeded in breaking the spell— he had turned away. A miserable disquietude and self-repulsion possessed him. He felt sick, body and soul. He had but one thought—to free himself once and for all from this unwarranted ordeal. Why should *he* have been singled out? What hint of any kind of "encouragement" had he been responsible for? Or was this ghostly encounter an experience that had been shared by other visitors to the old bookseller's sanctum—maybe less squeamish than himself? His chilled bloodless fingers clenched on the open page of the book beneath them. He strove in vain to master himself, to fight the thing out. It was as if an icy hand had him in its grip, daring him to stir.

The evening wind had died with the fading day. The three poplars, every budded double-curved twig outlined against the glassy grey of the west, stood motionless.

Daylight, even dusk was all very well, but supposing this presence, as the dark drew on, ventured a little nearer? And suddenly his alarms—as much now of the body as of the mind—were over. She had been interrupted.

A footstep had sounded in the corridor. Alan started to his feet. The handle of the door had turned in the old brass lock; he watched it. With a jerk he twisted his head on his shoulders. He was alone. Yet again the interrupter had rattled impatiently with the door handle. Alan at last managed to respond to the summons. But even as he grasped the handle on his own side of it, the door was pushed open against him and a long bearded face peered through.

"Pardon," said this stranger, "I didn't realize you had locked yourself in."

In the thin evening twilight that was now their only illumination Alan found himself blushing like a schoolgirl.

"But I hadn't," he stammered. "Of course not. The catch must have jammed. I came in here myself only a few minutes ago."

The long face with its rather watery blue-grey eyes placidly continued to survey him in the dusk. "And yet, you know," its owner drawled, with a *soupçon* of incredulity, "I should have guessed myself that I have been poking about in our patron's shop out there for at least the best part of half an hour. But that, of course, is one of the charms of lit-er-a-ture. You haven't chanced, I suppose, on a copy of the *Vulgar Errors*—Sir Thomas Browne?"

Alan shook his head. "The Bs I think are in that corner," he replied, "—alphabetical. But I didn't notice the *Errors*."

Nor did he stay to help his fellow-customer find the volume. He hurried out, and this time he had no spoil to present to the old bookseller in recognition of the rent due for his occupation of the parlour.

A whole week went by, its last few days the battleground of a continuous conflict of mind. He hadn't, he assured himself with the utmost conviction, the faintest desire in the world to set eyes again on—on what he *had* set eyes on. That was certain. It had been the oddest of shocks to what he had thought about things, to what had gone before, and, yes, to his vanity. Besides, the more he occupied himself with and pondered over his peculiar little experience the more probable it seemed that it and she and everything connected with her had been nothing but a cheat of the senses, a triumph of self-deception—a pure illusion, induced by the quiet, the solitude, the stirrings of springtime at the window, the feeling of age in the room, the romantic associations—and last, to the Herrick!

All this served very well in the middle of the morning or at two o'clock in the afternoon. But a chance waft of the year's first waxen hyacinths, the onset of evening, a glimpse of the waning moon—at any such oblique reminder of what had happened, these pretty arguments fell flat as a house of cards. Illusion! Then why had everything else in his life become by comparison so empty of interest and himself at a loose end? The thought of Mr. Elliott's bookshop at such moments was like an hypnotic lure. Cheat himself as he might, he knew it was only cheating. Distrust the fowler as he might, he knew what nets he was in. How gross a folly to be at the mercy of one vehement coupling of glances. If only it had been that other face! And yet, supposing he were wrong about all this; supposing this phantasm really was in need of help, couldn't rest, had come back for something—there *were* things one might want to come back for—and even for something which he alone could give?

What wonder this restless conflict of mind reacted on his body and broke his sleep? Naturally a little invalidish in his appetite, Alan now suffered the pangs of a violent attack of indigestion. And at last he could endure himself no longer. On the following Tuesday he once more pushed open the outer door of Mr. Elliott's bookshop, with its jangling bell, and entered, hot and breathless, from out of the pouring rain.

"There was a book I caught sight of," he panted out to the old gentleman as he came in, "when I was here last, you know. In the other room. I won't keep you a minute."

At this, the bookseller's bland eye fixed itself an instant on the fair flushed face, almost as if he too could a tale unfold.

"Let me take your umbrella, sir," he entreated. "Sopping! A real downpour. But very welcome to the farmers, I'll be bound—if for once in a while they'd only *say* so. No hurry whatever, sir."

Downpour indeed it was. As Alan entered the parlour the cold sullen gush of rain on the young lilac buds and cobble-stones of the little yard in the dreary leaden light at the window resounded steadily on. He had set out in the belief that his one desire was to prove that his "ghost" was no ghost at all, that he had been a victim of a pure hallucination. Yet throughout his journey, with only his umbrella for company, he had been conscious of a thrill of excitement and expectation. And now that he had closed the door behind him, and had shut himself in, the faded little room in this obscurity at once began to influence his mind in much the same fashion as the livid gloom of an approaching thunderstorm affects the scenery of the hills and valleys over which it broods.

And this, it soon seemed, was to be his sole reward! His excitement fizzled out.

With every passing moment his heart fell lower. He had gone away filled with a stark irrational hatred of the poor restless phantasmal creature who had intruded on his solitude. He had come back only to realize not only that she herself had been his lodestone, but that, even though any particular spot may undoubtedly be "haunted," it by no means follows that its ghost is always at home. Everything about him seemed to have changed a little. Or was the change only in himself? In this damp air the room smelt of dry-rot and mouldering leather. Even the pretty grate looked thicklier scurfed with rust. And the books on the shelves had now taken to themselves the leaden livery of the weather. "Look not too closely on us," they seemed to cry. "What are we all but memorials of the dead? And we too are swiftly journeying towards the dust."

The prospect from the window was even more desolating. None the less Alan continued to stare stupidly out of it. By the time he had turned away again he had become certain—though how he couldn't tell—that he need have no apprehension whatever of intangible company today. Mr. Elliott's "parlour" was emptier than he supposed a room could be. It seemed as if by sheer aversion for its late inmate he had exorcized it, and, irrational creature that he was, a stab of regret followed.

He turned to go. He gave a last look round—and paused. Was it that the skies had lightened a little or had he really failed to notice at his entry that the door at which his visitor had appeared was a few inches open? He stepped across softly and glanced up the staircase. Only vacancy there too. But that door was also ajar. The two faint daylights from above and below mingled midway. For a moment or two be hesitated. The next he had stolen swiftly and furtively up the staircase and had looked in.

This room was not only empty but abandoned. It was naked of any stick of furniture and almost of any trace of human occupation. Yet with its shallow bow window, low ceiling, and morning sun it must once in its heyday have blossomed like the rose. The flowered paper on its walls was dingy now: a few darker squares and oblongs alone showed where pictures had once hung. The brass gas bracket was green with verdigris, and a jutting rod was the only evidence of the canopy where once a bed had been.

But even vacancy may convey a sense of age and tell its tale. Alan was looking into the past. Indeed, the stale remnant of some once pervasive perfume still hung in the musty atmosphere of the room, though its sole refuse consisted of a few dust-grimed books in a corner and—on a curved white narrow shelf that winged the minute fireplace—a rusty hairpin.

Alan stooped, and very gingerly, with gloved finger and thumb, turned the books over—a blistered green-bound *Enoch Arden*, a small thick copy of *The Mysteries of Paris*, Dante Gabriel Rossetti's *House of Life*, a *Nightingale Valley*, a few damp fly-blown shockers, some of them in French and paper-bound; and last, a square black American cloth-bound exercise book with *E.F.* cut out with a clumsy penknife at one of the top corners. The cockled cloth was slightly greened.

He raised the cover with the extreme tips of his fingers, stooped forward a little, and found himself in the window-light scanning with peculiar intensity the vanishing lineaments of a faded photograph—the photograph of a young woman in clothes somehow made the more old-fashioned in appearance by the ravages of time and light on the discoloured cardboard. He knew this face; and yet not *this* face. For days past it had not been out of his mind for more than a few hours together. But while his first impression had been that of the vivid likeness of the one to the other, what next showed clearest were the differences between them. Differences that stirred his heart into a sudden tumult.

The hair in the photograph was dressed in pretty much the same fashion—drawn up and back from the narrow temples across the widening head. The lips were, possibly, not so full; certainly not so dark. And though the cheek oven of this much younger face was a little sunken, these faded eyes—a fading only of the paper

depicting them and not of age—looked out at him without the faintest trace of boldness or effrontery. They were, it is true, fixed profoundly on his own. But they showed no interest in him, little awareness, no speculation—only a remote settled melancholy. What strange surmises, the young man reflected, must the professional photographer at times indulge in when from beneath his ink-black inquisitorial velvet cowl he peers into his camera at a face as careless of human curiosity as this had been. The young woman in the photograph had made, if any, a more feeble attempt to conceal her secret sorrows than a pall to conceal its bier or a broken sepulchre its bones.

At a breath the young man's aversion had died away. A shame-stricken compassion of which he had never dreamed himself capable had swept over him in its stead. He gazed on for a minute or two at the photograph—this withering memento which not even the removing men seemed to have considered worth flinging into a dustbin; then he opened the book at random—towards the middle of it—and leaning into the light at the window read these lines:

My midnight lamp burns dim with shame,
　In Heaven the moon is low;
Sweet sharer of its secret flame,
　Arise, and go!

Haste, for dawn's envious gaping grave
　Bids thee not linger here;
Though gone is all I am, and have—
　Thy ghost once absent, dear.

He read them over again, then glanced stealthily up and out. They were a voice from the dead. It was as if he had trespassed into the echoing cold of a vault. And as he looked about him he suddenly realized that at any moment he might be interrupted, caught—prying. With a swift glance over his shoulder he pushed the photograph back into the old exercise book, and tucking this under his arm beneath his coat, tiptoed down the unlighted stairs into the parlour.

It had been a bold venture—at least for Alan. For, of all things in this world he disliked, he disliked by far the most being caught out in any little breach of the conventions. Suppose that old cod-like Mrs. Elliott had caught him exploring this abandoned bedroom? After listening yet again for any rumour either of herself or of her husband, he drew out from the lowest shelf nearby two old sheepskin folios, seated himself in full view of the door that led into the shop, and having hidden the exercise book well within cover of these antiquated tomes he began to turn over its pages. The trick took him back to his early school days—the sun, the heat, the drone of bees at the window, a settling wayward fly, the tick of the clock on the wall, and the penny "blood" half concealed in his arithmetic book. He smiled to himself. Wasn't he being kept in now? And how very odd he should be minding so little what, only an hour before, he had foreseen he would be minding so much. How do ghosts *show* that you needn't expect them? Not even in their chosen haunts?

The book he was now examining was not exactly a penny "blood." In spite of appearances it must have cost at least sixpence. The once black ink on it pages had faded, and mildew dappled the leaves. The handwriting was irregular, with protracted loops. And what was written in the book consisted of verses, interlarded with occasional passages in prose, and a day or a date here and there, and all set down apparently just as it had taken the writer's fancy. And since many of the verses were heavily corrected and some of them interlined, Alan concluded—without any very unusual acumen!—that they were homemade. Moreover, on evidence as flimsy as this, he had instantly surmised who this E.F. was, and that here was not only her book, but a book of her own authorship. So completely, too, had his antipathy to the writer of it now vanished out of memory, so swiftly had the youthful, tragic face in the photograph secreted itself in his sentiments, that he found himself reading these scribbled "effusions" with a mind all but bereft of its critical faculties. And of these the young man had hitherto rather boasted himself.

Still, poetry, good or bad, depends for its very life on the hospitable reader, as tinder awaits the spark. After that, what else matters? The flame leaps, the bosom glows! And as Alan read on he never for an instant doubted that here, however faultily expressed, was what the specialist is apt to call "a transcript of life." He knew of old—how remotely of old it now seemed—what feminine wiles are capable of; but here, surely, was the truth of self to self. He had greedily and yet with real horror looked forward to his reappearance here, as if Mr. Elliott's little parlour was the positive abode of the Evil One. And yet now that he was actually pecking about beneath the very meshes of his nets, he was drinking in those call-notes as if they were cascading down upon him out of the heavens from the throat of Shelley's skylark itself. For what is Time to the artifices of Eros? Had he not (with Chaucer's help) once fallen head over ears in love with the faithless Criseyde? He drank in what he had begun to read as if his mind wore a wilderness thirsty for rain, though the pall of cloud that darkened the window behind him was supplying it in full volume. He was elated and at the same time dejected at the thought that he was perhaps the very first human creature, apart from the fountain-head, to sip of these secret waters.

And he had not read very far before he realized that its contents referred to an actual experience as well as to one of the imagination. He realized too that the earlier poems had been written at rather long intervals; and, though he doubted very much if they were first attempts, that their technique tended to improve as they went on—at least, that of the first twenty poems or so. With a small ivory pocket paper-knife which he always carried about with him he was now delicately separating page 12 from page 13, and he continued to read at random:

> There was sweet water once,
>   Where in my childhood I
> Watched for the happy innocent nonce
>   Day's solemn clouds float by.
>
> O age blur not that glass;
>   Kind Heaven still shed thy rain;

Even now sighs shake me as I pass
  Those gentle haunts again.

He turned over the page:

Lullay, my heart, and find thy peace
  Where thine old solitary pastures lie;
Their light, their dews need never cease,
  Nor sunbeams from on high.

Lullay, and happy dream, nor roam,
  Wild though the hills may shine,
Once there, thou soon would'st long for home,
  As I for mine!

and then:

Do you see; O, do you see?—
  Speak—and some inward self that accent
    knows
  Bidding the orient East its rose disclose—
And daybreak wake in me.

Do you hear? O, do you hear?—
  This heart whose pulse like menacing
    night-bird cries?

> *Dark, utter dark, my loved, is in these eyes*
> *When gaunt good-bye draws near.*

and then, after a few more pages:

> *"There is a garden in her face:"*
> *My face! Woe's me were that my all!—*
> *Nay, but my self, though thine its grace,*
> *Thy fountain is, thy peach-bloomed wall.*
>
> *Come soon that twilight dusky hour,*
> *When thou thy self shalt enter in*
> *And take thy fill of every flower,*
> *Since thine they have always been.*
>
> *No rue? No myrrh? No nightshade? Oh,*
> *Tremble not, spirit! All is well.*
> *For Love's is that lovely garden; and so,*
> *There only pleasures dwell.*

Turning over the limp fusty leaves, one by one, he browsed on:

> *When you are gone, and I'm alone,*
> *From every object that I see*
> *Its secret source of life is flown:*

All things look cold and strange to me.

Even what I use—my rings, my gloves,
My parasol, the clothes I wear—
"Once she was happy; now she loves!
Once young," they cry, "now carked with care!"

I wake and watch, when the moon is here—
A shadow tracks me on. And I—
Darker than any shadow—fear
Her fabulous inconsistency.

That sphinx, the Future, marks its prey;
I who was ardent, sanguine, free,
Starve now in fleshly cell all day—
And yours the rusting key.

And then:

Your maddening face befools my eyes,
Your hand—I wake to feel—
Lost in deep midnight's black surmise—
Its touch my veins congeal!

What peace for me in star or moon?
What solace in nightingale!

They tell me of the lost and gone—
And dawn completes the tale.

A note in pencil—the point of which must have broken in use—followed at the foot of the page:

"All this means all but *nothing* of what was in my mind when I began to write it. *Dawn!!* I look at it, read it—it is like a saucer of milk in a cage full of asps. I didn't *know* one's mind could dwell only on one thought, one face, one longing, on and on without any respite, and yet remain sane. I didn't even know—until when?—it was possible to be happy, unendurably happy, and yet as miserable and as hopeless as a devil in hell. It is as if I were sharing my own body with a self I hate and fear and shake in terror at, and yet am powerless to be rid of. Well, never mind. If I *can* go on, that's my business. They mouth and talk and stare and sneer at me. What do I care! The very leaves of the trees whisper against me, and last night came thunder. I see my haunted face in every stone. And what cares *he*! Why should he? Would *I*, if I were a man? I sit here alone in the evening—waiting. My heart is a quicksand biding its time to swallow me up. Yet it isn't even that I question now whether he ever loved me or not— I only thirst and thirst for him to come. One look, a word, and I am at peace again. At peace! And yet I wonder sometimes, if I—if it is ever *conceivable* that I still love him. Does steel love the magnet? Surely that moon which shone last night with her haggard glare in both our faces *abhors* the earth from which, poor wretch, she parted to perish and yet from which she can never, never, never utterly break away? Never, never, never. Oh God, how tired I am!—knowing as I do—as if my life were all being lived over again—that only worse lies in wait for me, that the more I feel the less I am able to please him. I *see* myself dragging on and on—and that other sinister mocking one within rises up and looks at me—'What? And shall *I* never come into my own!'"

Alan had found some little difficulty in deciphering the faint, blurred, pencilled handwriting—he decided to come back to this page again, then turned it over and read on:

Your hate I see, and can endure, nay, must—
Endure the stark denial of your love;
It is your silence, like a cankering rust,
That I am perishing of.

What reck you of the blinded hours I spend
Crouched on my knees beside a shrouded bed?
Grief even for the loveliest has an end;
No end in one whose soul it is lies dead.

I watch the aged who've dared the cold slow ice
That creeps from limb to limb, from sense to sense,
Yet never dreamed this also is the price
Which youth must pay for a perjured innocence.

Yours that fond lingering lesson. Be content!
Not one sole moment of its course I rue.
The all I had was little. Now it's spent.
Spit on the empty purse; 'tis naught to you.

And then these 'Lines on Ophelia':

She found an exit from her life;
She to an earthly green-room sped
Where parched-up souls distraught with strife
Sleep and are comforted.

Hamlet! I know that dream-drugged eye,
That self-coiled melancholic mien!
Hers was a happy fate—to die:
Mine—her foul Might-have-been.

and then:

To-morrow waits me at my gate,
While all my yesterdays swarm near;
And one mouth whines, Too late, too late:
And one is dumb with fear.

Was this the all that life could give
Me—who from cradle hungered on,
Body and soul aflame, to live—
Giving my all—and then be gone?

O sun in heaven, to don that shroud,
When April's cuckoo thrilled the air!
Light thou no more the fields I loved.
Be only winter there!

and then:

> *Have done with moaning, idiot heart;*
> *If it so be that Love has wings*
> *I with my shears will find an art*
> *To still his flutterings.*

> *Wrench off that bandage too will I,*
> *And show the imp he is blind indeed;*
> *Hot irons shall prove my mastery;*
> *He shall not weep, but bleed.*

> *And when he is dead, and cold as stone,*
> *Then in his Mother's book I'll con*
> *The lesson none need learn alone,*
> *And, callous as she, play on.*

He raised his eyes. The heavy rain had ebbed into a drifting drizzle; the day had darkened. He stared vacantly for a moment or two out of the rain-drenched window, and then, turning back a few of the damp cockled leaves, once more resumed his reading:

> *And when at last I journey where*
> *All thought of you I must resign,*

Will the least memory of me be fair,
Or will you even my ghost malign?

I plead for nothing. Nay, Time's tooth—
That frets the very soul away—
May prove at last your slanders truth,
And me the Slut you say.

There followed a series of unintelligible scrawls. It was as if the writer had been practising a signature in various kinds of more or less affected handwritings: Esther de Bourgh, Esther de Bourgh, Esther De Bourgh, E. de Bourgh, E de B, E de B, E de Ice Bourgh, Esther de la Ice Bourgh, Esther de Borgia, Esther Cesarina de Borgia, Esther de Bauch, Esther de Bausch, E de Bosh. And then, this unfinished scrap:

Why cheat the heart with old deceits?—
Love—was it love in thine
Could leave me thus grown sick of sweets
And...

The words sounded on—forlornly and even a little self-pityingly—in Alan's mind.

Sick of sweets, sick of sweets. He had had enough for to-day. He shut the book, lifted his head, and with a shuddering yawn and a heavy frown on his young face, once more stared out of the window.

This E.F., whoever she was, had often sat in this room, alert, elated, drinking in its rosily reflected morning sunshine from that wall, happy even in being merely herself young, alone, and alive. He could even watch in fancy that intense lowered face as she stitched steadily on, lost in a passionate reverie, while she listened to as dismal a downpour as that which had but lately ceased on the moss-grown cobbles under the window. "It's only one's inmost *self* that matters," she had scribbled at the end of one of her rhymes. And then—how long afterwards?—the days, empty of everything but that horror and dryness of the heart, when desire had corrupted and hope was gone, and every hour of solitude must have seemed to be lying in wait only to prove the waste, the bleakness, the desolation to which the soul within can come. No doubt in time they would learn even a bookworm to be a worm. "That is one of the charms of lit-er-a-ture," as the bland, bearded, supercilious gentleman had expressed it. But he wouldn't have sentimentalized about it.

Oddly enough, it hadn't yet occurred to Alan to speculate what kind of human being it was to whom so many of these poems had been addressed, and to whom seemingly every one of them had clearer or vaguer reference. There are ghosts for whom spectre is the better word. In this, the gloomiest hour of an English spring, he glanced again at the door he had shut behind him in positive hope that it might yet open once more—that he was not so utterly alone as he seemed. Sick: sick: surely, surely a few years of life could not have wreaked such horrifying changes in any human face and spirit as that!

But the least promising method apparently of evoking a visitant from another world is to wait on to welcome it. Better, perhaps, postpone any little experiment of this kind until after the veils of nightfall have descended. Not that he had failed to notice how overwhelming is the evidence that when once you have gone from this world you have gone for ever. Still, even if he *had* been merely the victim of an illusion, it would have been something just to smile or to nod in a common friendly human fashion, to lift up the dingy little black exercise book in his hand, merely to show that its owner had not confided in him in vain.

He was an absurdly timid creature—tongue-tied when he wanted most to express himself. And yet, if only... His glance strayed from door to book again. It was curious that the reading of poems like these should yet have proved a sort of solace. They had triumphed even over the miserable setting destiny had bestowed on them. Surely lit-er-a-ture without any vestige of merit in it couldn't do that. A veil of day-dream drew over the fair and rather effeminate face. And yet the young man was no longer merely brooding; he was beginning to make plans. And he was making them without any help from the source from which it might have been expected.

Seeming *revenants*, of course, in this busy world are not of much account. They make indelible impressions if they do chance to visit one, though it is imprudent perhaps to share them with the sceptic. None the less at this moment he was finding it almost impossible to recall the face not of the photograph but of his phantasm. And though there was nothing in the earlier poems he had read to suggest that they could not have been the work of the former, was it conceivable that they could ever have been the work of— that other one? But why not! To judge from some quite famous poets' faces, their owners would have flourished at least as successfully in the pork-butchering line. Herrick himself—well, he was not exactly ethereal in appearance. But what need for these ridiculous unanswerable questions? Whoever *E.F.* had been, and whatever the authorship of the poems, he himself could at least claim now to be their only rebegetter.

At this thought a thrill of excitement had run through Alan's veins. Surely the next best thing to publishing a first volume of verse of one's own—and that he had now decided never to attempt—is to publish someone else's. He had seen worse stuff than this in print, and on hand-made paper too.

'Why shouldn't he turn editor? How could one tell for certain that it is impossible to comfort—or, for that matter, to soothe the vanity—of some poor soul simply because it has happened to set out on the last long journey a few years before oneself? Mere initials are little short of anonymity, and even kindred spirits may be all the kinder if kept at the safe distance which anonymity ensures. But what about the old bookseller? An Englishman's shop is his castle, and this battered old exercise book, Alan assumed, must fully as much as any other volume on the shelves around him be the legal property of the current tenant of the house. Or possibly the ground-landlord's? He determined to take Mr. Elliott into his confidence—but very discreetly.

With this decision, he got up—dismayed to discover that it was now a full half-hour after closing time. None the less he found the old bookseller sitting at his table and apparently lost to the cares of business beneath a wire-protected gas-bracket now used for an electric bulb. The outer door was still wide open, and the sullen clouds of the last of evening seemed to have descended even more louringly over the rain-soaked streets. A solitary dog loped by the shrouded entrance. Not a sound pierced the monotony of the drizzle.

"I wonder," Alan began, keeping the inflexions of his voice well in check, "I wonder if you have ever noticed *this* particular book? It is in manuscript… Verse."

"Verse, sir?" said the bookseller, fumbling in a tight waistcoat pocket for the silver case of his second pair of spectacles. "Well, now, verse—in manuscript. *That* doesn't sound as if it's likely to be of much value, though finds there have been, I grant you. Poems and sermons—we are fairly glutted out with them nowadays; still, there was this Omar Khayyám fuss, sir, so you never know."

He adjusted his spectacles and opened the book where the book opened itself. Alan stooped over the old man's shoulder and read with him:

Once in kind arms, alas, you held me close;
Sweet to its sepals was the unfolding rose.
Why, then—though wind-blown, hither, thither,

I languish still, rot on, and wither
Yet live, God only knows.

A queer, intent, an almost hunted expression drew over Mr. Elliott's greyish face as he read on.

"Now I wonder," he said at last, firmly laying the book down again and turning an eye as guileless as an infant's to meet Alan's scrutiny, "I wonder now who could have written that? Not that I flatter myself to be much of a judge. I leave that to my customers, sir."

"There is an *E.F.* cut out on the corner," said Alan, "and," the words came with difficulty, "there is a photograph inside. But then I suppose," he added hastily, automatically putting out his hand for the book and withdrawing it again, "I suppose just a loose photograph doesn't prove anything. Not at least to whom it belonged—the book, I mean."

"No, sir," said the bookseller, as if he thoroughly enjoyed little problems of this nature; "in a manner of speaking I suppose it don't." But he made no attempt to find the photograph, and a rather prolonged pause followed.

"It's quiet in that room in there," Alan managed to remark at last. "Extraordinarily quiet. You haven't yourself, I suppose, ever noticed the book before?"

Mr. Elliott removed both pairs of spectacles from the bridge of his nose. "Quiet is the word, sir," he replied, in a voice suiting the occasion. "And it's quieter yet in the two upper rooms above it. Especially of a winter's evening. Mrs. Elliott and me don't use that part of the house much, though there is a good bit of lumber stowed away in the nearest of 'em. We can't sell more than a fraction of the books we get, sir, so we store what's over up there for the pulpers. I doubt if I have even so much as seen the inside of the other room these six months past. As a matter of fact," he pursed his mouth and nodded, "what with servant-girls and the like, and not everybody being as common-sensical as most, we don't mention it much."

The bookseller's absent eye was now fixed on the rain-soaked street, and Alan waited, leaving his "What?" unsaid.

"You see, sir, the lady that lived with Dr. Marchmont here—his niece, or ward or whatever it may be—well, they say she came to what they call an untimely end. A love affair. But there, for the matter of that you can't open your evening newspaper without finding more of such things than you get in a spring season's fiction. Strychnine, sir—that was the way of it; and it isn't exactly the poison I myself should choose for the purpose. It erects up the body like an arch, sir. So." With a gesture of his small square hand Mr. Elliott pictured the effect in the air. "Dr. Marchmont hadn't much of a practice by that time, I understand; but I expect he came to a pretty sudden standstill when he saw *that* on the bed. A tall man, sir, with a sharp nose."

Alan refrained from looking at the bookseller. His eyes stayed fixed on the doorway which led out into the world beyond, and they did not stir. But he had seen the tall dark man with the sharp nose as clearly as if he had met him face to face, and was conscious of a repulsion far more deadly than the mere features would seem to warrant. And yet; *why* should he have come to a "standstill" quite like that if... But the bookseller had opened the fusty mildewed book at another page. He sniffed, then having rather pernicketily adjusted his spectacles, read over yet another of the poems:

Esther! *came whisper from my bed.*
Answer me, Esther—are you there?
'Twas waking self to self that's dead
Called on the empty stair.

Stir not that pit; she is lost and gone,
A Jew decoyed her to her doom.
Sullenly knolls her passing bell
Mocking me in the gloom.

The old man gingerly turned the leaf, and read on:

Last evening, as I sat alone—
Thimble on finger, needle and thread—
Light dimming as the dusk drew on,
  I dreamed that I was dead.

Like wildering timeless plains of snow
Which bitter winds to ice congeal
The world stretched far as sight could go
  'Neath skies as hard as steel.

Lost in that nought of night I stood
And watched my body—brain and breast
In dreadful anguish—in the mould
   Grope to'rd its final rest.

Its craving dreams of sense dropped down
Like crumbling maggots in the sod:
Spectral, I stood; all longing gone,
   Exiled from hope and God.

And you I loved, who once loved me,
And shook with pangs this mortal frame,
Were sunk to such an infamy
   That when I called your name,

Its knell so racked that sentient clay
That my lost spirit lurking near,
Wailed, like the damned, and fled away—
   And woke me, stark with Fear.

He pondered a moment, turned back the leaf again, and holding the book open with his dumpy forefinger, "A *Jew* now," he muttered to himself, "I never heard any mention of a Jew. But what, if you follow me," he added, tapping on the open page with his spectacles, "what I feel about such things as these is that they're not so much what may be called mournful as *morbid*, sir. They rankle. I don't say, mind you, there isn't a ring of truth in them— but it's so *put*, if you follow me, as to make it worse. Why, if all our little mistakes were dealt with in such a vengeful spirit as this—as *this*, where would any of us be? And death... Say things out, sir, by all means. But what things? It isn't human nature, And what's more," he finished pensively, "I haven't noticed that the stuff *sells* much the better for it."

Alan had listened but had not paid much attention to these moralizings. "You mean," he said, "that you think the book *did* actually belong to the lady who lived here, and that—that it was she herself who wrote the poems? But then you see it's *E.F.* on the cover, and I thought you said the name was Marchmont?"

'Yes, sir, Marchmont. Between you and me, there was a Mrs., I understand; but she went away. And who this young woman was I don't rightly know. Not much good, I fancy. At least..." he emptily eyed again the blurred lettering of the poem. "But there, sir," he went on with decision, "there's no need that I can see to worry about that. The whole thing's a good many years gone, and what consequence is it now? You'd be astonished how few of my customers really care who wrote a book so long as wrote it was. Which is not to suggest that if we get someone—someone with a name, I mean—to lay out the full story of the young woman as a sort of foreword, there might not be money in it. There *might* be. It doesn't much signify nowadays what you say about the dead, not legally, I mean. And especially these poets, sir. It all goes in under 'biography.' Besides, a suicide's a suicide all the world over. On the other hand—" and he glanced over his shoulder, "I rather fancy Mrs. E. wouldn't care to be mixed up in the affair. What she reads she never much approves of, though that's the kind of reading she likes best. The ladies can be so very scrupulous."

Alan had not seen the old bookseller in quite so bright a light as this before.

"What I was wondering, Mr. Elliott," he replied in tones so frigid they suggested he was at least twenty years older than he appeared to be, "is whether you would have any objection to my sending the book myself to the printers. It's merely an idea. One can't tell. It could do no harm. Perhaps who*ever* it was who wrote the poems may have hoped some day to get them printed—you never know. It would be at my expense, of course. I shouldn't dream of taking a penny piece and I would rather there were no introduction—by *any* one. There need be no name or address on the title page, need there? But this is of course only if you see no objection?"

Mr. Elliott had once more lifted by an inch or two the back cover of the exercise book, as if possibly in search of the photograph. He found only this pencilled scrawl:

Well, well, well! squeaked the kitten to the cat;
Mousie refuses to play any more! so that's
the end of that!

He shut up the book and rested his small plump hand on it.

"I suppose, sir," he inquired discreetly, "there *isn't* any risk of any infringement of copyright? I mean," he added, twisting round his unspectacled face a little in Alan's direction, "there isn't likely to be anybody who would *recognize* what's in here? I am not of course referring to the photograph, but a book, even nowadays, may be what you may call *too* true spoken—when it's new, I mean. And it's not so much Mrs. E. I have in mind now as the police," he whispered the word—"the *police*."

Alan returned his blurred glance without flinching.

"Oh, no…" he said. "Besides I should merely put *E.F.* on the title page and say it had been printed privately. I am quite prepared to take the risk."

The cold tones of the young man seemed to have a little daunted the old bookseller.

"Very well, sir. I will have just a word with a young lawyer friend of mine, and if that's all right, why, sir, you are welcome."

"And the books could be sold from here?"

"'Sold?' Why, yes, sir—they'll have plenty of respectable company, at any rate."

But if Alan had guilelessly supposed that the mere signing of a cheque for £33 10s. in settlement of a local printer's account would finally exile a ghost that now haunted his mind far more persistently than it could ever have haunted Mr. Elliott's green parlour, he soon discovered his mistake. He had kept the photograph, but had long since given up any attempt to find his way through the maze in which he found himself. Why, why should he concern himself with what an ill-starred life had done to that young face? If the heart, if the very soul is haunted by a ghost, need one heed the frigid dictates of the mind? Infatuated young man, he was in servitude to one who had left the world years before he was born, and had left it, it seemed, only the sweeter by her exit. He was sick for love of one who was once alive but was now dead, and—why should he deny it? Mrs. E. wouldn't!—damned.

Still, except by way of correspondence he avoided Mr. Elliott and his parlour for weeks, until in fact the poems were finally in print, until their neat grey deckled paper covers had been stitched on, and the copies were ready for a clamorous public! So it was early one morning in the month of June before he once more found himself in the old bookseller's quiet annexe. The bush of lilac, stirred by the warm languid breeze at the window, was shaking free its faded once-fragrant tassels of bloom and tapering heart-shaped leaves from the last dews of night. The young poplars stood like gold-green torches against the blue of the sky. A thrush was singing somewhere out of sight. It was a scene worthy of Arcady.

Alan had trailed through life without any positive need to call on any latent energy he might possess. And now that he had seen through the press his first essay in publishing a reaction had set in. A cloud of despondency shadowed his young features as he stared out through the glass of the window. Through the weeks gone by he had been assuring himself that it was no more than an act of mere decency to get the poems into print. A vicarious thirty pounds or so, just to quiet his conscience. What reward was even thinkable? And yet but a few nights before he had found himself sitting up in bed in the dark of the small hours just as if there had come a tap upon the panel of his door or a voice had summoned him out of dream. He had sat up, leaning against his bed-rail, exhausted by his

few hours' broken sleep. And in the vacancy of his mind had appeared yet again in silhouette against the dark the living presentment of the young face of the photograph. Merely the image of a face floating there, with waxen downcast lids, the features passive as those of a death-mask—as unembodied an object as the afterimage of a flower. There was no speculation in the downcast eyes, and in that lovely longed-for face; no, nothing whatever for *him*—and it had faded out as a mirage of green-fronded palm trees and water fades in the lifeless sands of the desert.

He hadn't any desire to sleep again that night. Dreams might come; and wakeful questions pestered him. How old was she when the first of the poems was written? How old when no more came, and she herself had gone on—gone on? That barren awful road of disillusionment, satiety, self-disdain. Had she even when young and untroubled ever been happy? Was what she had written even true? How far are poems *true*? What had really happened? What had been left out? You can't even tell—yourself—what goes on in the silent places of your mind when you have swallowed, so to speak, the dreadful outside things of life. What, for example, had *Measure for Measure* to do with the author of *Venus and Adonis*, and what *Don Juan* with Byron as a child? One thing, young women of his own day didn't take their little affairs like that. They kept life in focus. But that ghost! The ravages, the point, the insidiousness, the very clothes!

Coming to that, then, who the devil had he been taking such pains over? The question kept hammering at his mind day after day; it was still unanswered, showed no promise of an answer. And the Arcadian scene beyond the windows suddenly became an irony and a jeer. The unseen bird itself sang on in vulgar mockery, 'Come *off* of it! Come off of it! Come off of it! Dolt, dolt, dolt!'

He turned away out of the brightness of the light, and fixed his eyes on the bulky brown paper package that contained the printed volumes. It was useless to stay here any longer. He would open the package, but merely to take a look at a copy and assure himself that no ingenuity of the printer had restored any little aberration of spelling or punctuation which he himself had corrected three times in the proofs. He knew the poems—or some of them—by heart now.

With extreme reluctance he had tried one or two of them on a literary friend— "An anonymous thing, you know, I came across it in an old book."

The friend had been polite rather than enthusiastic. After, cigarette between fingers, idly listening to a few stanzas, he had smiled and asked Alan if he had ever read a volume entitled *Poems of Currer, Ellis and Acton Bell.*

"Well, there you are! A disciple of Acton's, dear boy, if you ask *me*. Stuff as common as blackberries!"

And Alan had welcomed the verdict. He didn't want to share the poems with anybody. If nobody bought them and nobody cared, what matter? All the better. And he wasn't being sentimental about them now either. He didn't care if they had any literary value or not. He had entrusted himself with them, and that was the end of the matter. What was Hecuba to him, or he to Hecuba? What?

And what did it signify that he had less right to the things even than Mrs. Elliott— who fortunately was never likely to stake out any claim. The moral ashbins old women can be, he thought bitterly. Simply because this forlorn young creature of the exercise book had been forced at last to make her exit from the world under the tragic but hardly triumphant arch of her own body, this old woman had put her hand over her mouth and looked "volumes" at that poor old hen-pecked husband of hers even at mention of her name. Suicides, of course, are a nuisance in any house. But all those years gone by! And what did they *know* the poor thing had done to merit their insults? *He* neither knew nor cared, yet for some obscure reason stead-ily wasted at least five minutes in untying the thick knotted cord of the parcel instead of chopping it up with his pocket knife in the indignant fashion which he had admired when he visited the printers.

The chastest little pile of copies was dis-closed at last in their grey-blue covers and with their enrichingly rough edges. The hand-made paper had been an afterthought.

A further cheque was ·due to the printer, but Alan begrudged not a farthing. He had even incited them to be expensive. He believed in turning things out nicely—even himself. He and his pretty volumes were "a pair!"

Having opened the parcel, having neatly folded up its prodigal wrappings of brown paper, and thrown away the padding and hanked the string, there was nothing further to do. He sat back in Mr. Elliott's old Windsor chair, leaning his chin on his knuckles. He was waiting, though he didn't confess it to himself. What he did confess to himself was that he was sick of it all. Age and life's usage may obscure, cover up, fret away a fellow creature at least as irrevocably as six feet of common clay.

When then he raised his eyes at some remote inward summons he was already a little hardened in hostility. He was looking clean across the gaily-lit room at its other occupant standing there in precisely the same attitude—the high-heeled shoe coquettishly arched on the lower of the three steps, the ridiculous flaunting hat, the eyes aslant beneath the darkened lids casting back on him their glitter from over a clumsy blur that was perfectly distinct on the cheek-bone in the vivid light of this June morning. And even this one instant's glimpse clarified and crystallized all his old horror and hatred. He knew that she had seen the tender first-fruits on the table. He knew that he had surprised a gleam of triumph in her snakish features, and he knew that she no more cared for that past self and its literary exercises than she cared for his silly greenhorn tribute to them. What then was she after?

The darkening glittering spectral eyes were once more communicating with him with immense rapidity, and yet were actually conveying about as empty or as mindless a message as eyes can. If half-extinguished fires in a dark room can be said to look coy, these did. But a coyness practised in a face less raddled and ravaged by time than by circumstance is not an engaging quality. "Arch!" My God, "arch" was the word!

Alan was shivering. How about the ravages that life's privy paw had made in his *own* fastidious consciousness? Had his own heart been a shade more faithful would the horror which he knew was now distorting his rather girlish features and looking out of his pale blue eyes have been quite so poisonously bitter?

Fortunately his back was turned to the window, and he could in part conceal his face with his hand before this visitor had had time to be fully aware what that face was saying. She had stirred. Her head was trembling slightly on her shoulders. Every tinily exquisite plume in the mauve ostrich feathers on her drooping hat trembled as if in sympathy. Her ringed fingers slipped down from the door to her narrow hip; her painted eyelids narrowed, as if she were about to speak to him. But at this moment there came a sudden flurry of wind in the lilac tree at the window, ravelling its dried-up flowers and silky leaves. She stooped, peered; and then, with a sharp, practised, feline, seductive nod, as bold as grass-green paint, she was gone. An instant or two, and in the last of that dying gust, the door above at the top of the narrow staircase, as if in a sudden access of bravado, violently slammed—'Touch me, tap at me, force me, if you dare!'

The impact shook the walls and rattled the windows of the room beneath. It jarred on the listener's nerves with the force of an imprecation. As abrupt a silence followed. Nauseated and slightly giddy he got up from his chair, resting his fingers automatically on the guileless pile of books, took up his hat, glanced vacantly at the gilded Piccadilly maker's name on the silk lining, and turned to go. As he did so, a woeful, shuddering fit of remorse swept over him, like a parched up blast of the sirocco over the sands of a desert. He shot a hasty strangulated look up the narrow empty staircase as he passed by. Then, "Oh God," he groaned to himself, "I wish—I *pray*—you poor thing, you could only be a little more at peace—whoever, wherever you are—whatever *I* am."

And then he was with the old book-seller again, and the worldly-wise old man was eyeing him as ingenuously as ever over his steel-rimmed glasses.

"He isn't looking quite himself," he was thinking. "Bless me, sir," he said aloud, "sit down and rest a bit. You must have been overdoing it. You look quite het up."

Alan feebly shook his head. His cheek was almost as colourless us the paper on which the poems had been printed; small beads of sweat lined his upper lip and damped his hair. He opened his mouth to reassure the old bookseller, but before he could utter a word they were both of them caught up and staring starkly at one another—like conspirators caught in the act. Their eyes met in glassy surmise. A low, sustained, sullen rumble had come sounding out to them from the remoter parts of the shop which Alan had but a moment before left finally behind him. The whole house shuddered as if at the menace of an earthquake.

"Bless my soul, sir!" cried the old bookseller. "What in merciful heaven was that!"

He hurried out, and the next instant stood in the entry of his parlour peering in through a dense fog of dust that now obscured the light of the morning. It silted softly down, revealing the innocent cause of the commotion. No irreparable calamity. It was merely that a patch of the old cracked plaster ceiling had fallen in, and a mass of rubble and plaster was now piled up, inches high, on the gate-leg table and the chair beside it, while the narrow laths of the ceiling above them, a few of which were splintered, lay exposed like the bones of a skeleton. A thick film of dust had settled over everything, intensifying with its grey veil the habitual hush of the charming little room. And almost at one and the same moment the old bookseller began to speculate first, what damages he might have been called upon to pay if his young customer had not in the nick of time vacated that chair, and next, that though perhaps his own little stock of the rare and the curious would be little worse for the disaster, Alan's venture might be very much so. Indeed, the few that were visible of the little pile of books—but that morning come virgin and speckless from the hands of the binders—were bruised and scattered. And as Mr. Elliott eyed them, his conscience smote him: "Softly now, softly," he muttered to himself, "or we shall have Mrs. E. down on this in pretty nearly no time!"

But Mrs. E. had not heard. No footfall sounded above; nothing stirred; all remained as it might be expected to remain. And Alan, who meanwhile had stayed motionless in the outer shop, at this moment joined the old bookseller, and looked in on the ruins.

"Well, there, sir," Mr. Elliott solemnly assured him, "all I can say is, it's a mercy you had come out of it. And by no more than a hair's breadth!"

But Alan made no answer. His mind was a void. He was listening again—and so intently that it might be supposed the faintest stirrings even on the uttermost out-skirts of the unseen might reach his ear. It was too late now—and in any case it hadn't occurred to him—to add to the title page of his volume that well-worn legend, "The heart knoweth his own bitterness; and a stranger doth not intermeddle with his joy." But it might at least have served for his own brief *apologia*. He had meant well—it would have suggested. You never can tell.

As they stood there, then, a brief silence had fallen on the ravaged room. And then a husky, querulous, censorious voice had broken out behind the pair of them: "Mr. E., where are you?"

alter de la Mare (1873 - 1956) was an English author, well-known for his book *Collected Stories for Children*.

Seth is the cartoonist behind the semi-annual hardback series of books, *Palookaville*.

His comics and drawings have appeared in *The New York Times*, *The Best American Comics*, *The Walrus*, *The New Yorker*, *The Globe and Mail*, and countless other publications. His latest graphic novel, *Clyde Fans* (twenty years in the making), will finally be published in the spring of 2019.

He is the subject of a documentary from the National Film Board of Canada, *Seth's Dominion*.

Seth lives in Guelph, Ontario, with his wife, Tania, and their two cats in an old house he has named "Inkwell's End."

Publisher's Note: 'The Green Room' was first published in 1925
in *Two Tales*.

Illustrations and design © Seth, 2018

Library and Archives Canada Cataloguing in Publication

De la Mare, Walter, 1873-1956, author
The green room / Walter De La Mare;
designed & decorated by Seth.

(Christmas ghost stories)
Short story.

Originally published: London : Bookman's Journal Office, 1925.

Issued in print and electronic formats.
ISBN 978-1-77196-257-5 (softcover).
ISBN 978-1-77196-258-2 (ebook)

I. Seth, 1962-, illustrator II. Title.

PR6007.E3G74 2018   823'.912   C2018-901749-X
                                      C2018-901750-3

Readied for the press by Daniel Wells
Illustrated and designed by Seth
Proofread by Emily Donaldson
Typeset by Chris Andrechek

PRINTED AND BOUND IN CANADA